Pebble Plus

Penguins!

ROCKHOPPER PENGUINS

by Jody S. Rake

PEBBLE
a capstone imprint

Pebble Plus is published by Pebble
1710 Roe Crest Drive, North Mankato, Minnesota 56003
www.mycapstone.com

Library of Congress Cataloging-in-Publication Data
Names: Rake, Jody Sullivan, author.
Title: Rockhopper penguins / by Jody S. Rake.
Description: North Mankato, Minnesota : Capstone, an imprint of Pebble, [2020] | Series: Pebble plus. Penguins! | Audience: Age 5-6. | Audience: K to Grade 3.
Identifiers: LCCN 2019008840 |
ISBN 9781977109392 (hardcover)
ISBN 9781977109453 (ebook PDF)
Subjects: LCSH: Eudyptes chrysocome--Juvenile literature.
Classification: LCC QL696.S473 R359 2020 | DDC 598.47--dc23
LC record available at https://lccn.loc.gov/2019008840

Editorial Credits

Donald Lemke, editor; Ted Williams, designer; Kelly Garvin, media researcher; Katy LaVigne, production specialist

Photo Credits

Minden Pictures: Jean-Paul Ferrero, 21, Hurgen and Christine Sohns, 11; Newscom/Michael Nolan/robertharding, 15; Shutterstock: Amplion, 6, Christian Rordam, 5, Designus, 6, Galyna Andrushko, 13, Gillian Santink, 17, JeremyRichards, 9, Ondrej Prosicky, cover, 19, sunsinger, 7, The Highland Rambler, 1

Design elements: Shutterstock/Rashad Ashur

Printed and bound in China.
1654

TABLE OF CONTENTS

FANCY FEATHERS

Rockhopper penguins are crested penguins. They have a bright yellow feather crest above their eyes. They have orange beaks and red eyes.

There are six different kinds of crested penguins. Rockhopper penguins are the smallest. They stand about 19 to 20 inches (48.3 to 50.8 centimeters) tall.

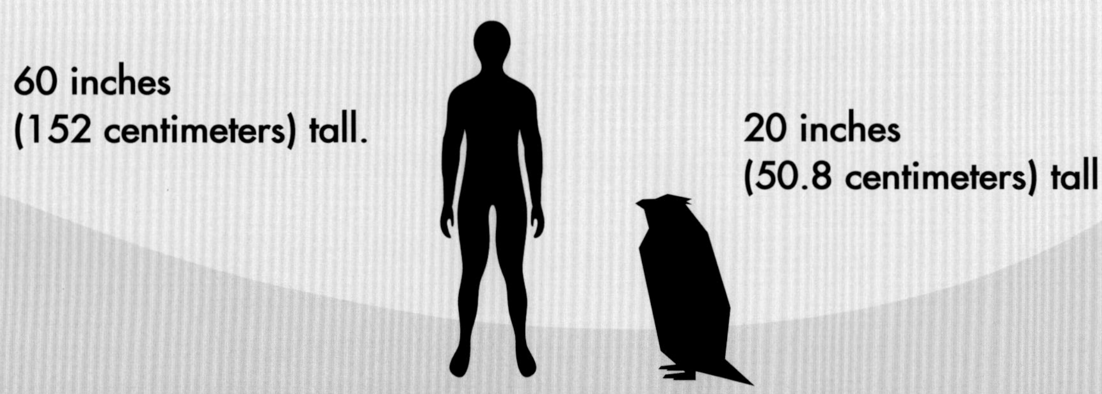

ROCK HOPPING

Rockhoppers live on rocky shores on islands near Antarctica, New Zealand, and South America. Rockhoppers don't waddle. They hop from rock to rock.

Rockhopper penguins can't fly. But they are great swimmers. They flap their flippers through the water and hunt for food. They eat krill, fish, and squid.

LUMPY NESTS AND FUZZY CHICKS

Rockhopper penguins spend months hunting at sea. In early spring they return to the rocky shore. Mother and father rockhoppers call to each other.

The rockhopper pair find a spot to build a nest. They build their nest out of dry seagrass and pebbles. They will use this spot the next time they build their nest.

Both parents keep the egg warm. It takes about one month for an egg to hatch. The chick is covered with fuzzy, warm down. Both parents care for the chick.

A ROCKHOPPER'S LIFE

When a rockhopper chick is about 10 weeks old it can take care of itself. It has grown waterproof feathers. Now it can swim and hunt.

Rockhoppers spend a lot of time hunting in the ocean. At the same time, killer whales, leopard seals, and sharks hunt rockhoppers. Rockhoppers live 10 to 15 years.

GLOSSARY

beak—the hard, front part of the mouth of birds

crest—a crown of pointed feathers on a bird's head; penguins with a crest are called crested

down—the soft, fluffy feathers of a baby bird

feather—one of the light, fluffy parts that cover a bird's body

flipper—one of the long, flat upper limbs of a penguin; flippers help penguins swim

krill—small, shrimp-like animal

seagrass—a type of plant that grows in the sea

waterproof—not allowing water to soak through

READ MORE

Rudolph, Jessica. *Rockhopper Penguin.* Weird but Cute. New York: Bearport Publishing, 2016.

Salomon, David. *Penguins!* Step into Reading. New York: Random House, 2017.

Schuh, Mari. *Penguins.* Black and White Animals. North Mankato, Minn.: Capstone Press, 2017.

INTERNET SITES

Kiddle: Rockhopper Penguin Facts
https://kids.kiddle.co/Rockhopper_penguin

PenguinWorld
www.penguinworld.com/types/rockhopper.html

KidZone: Penguins
https://www.kidzone.ws/animals/penguins/

CRITICAL THINKING QUESTIONS

1. How do rockhoppers move on land?
2. What do rockhopper penguins use to make their nests?
3. What animals hunt rockhopper penguins?

INDEX